POKÉMON

PIKACHU'S

RESCUE ADVENTURE

POKÉMON

PIKACHU'S

RESCUE ADVENTURE

ADAPTED BY
TRACEY WEST

SCHOLASTIC INC.

New York   Toronto   London   Auckland   Sydney
Mexico City   New Delhi   Hong Kong

ISBN 0-439-19969-7

12 11 10 9 8 7 6 5 4 3 2 1   1 2 3 4 5 6/0

Printed in the U.S.A.
First Scholastic printing, July 2000

CONTENTS

Meet the New Pokémon!

Meet the New Pokémon!

Hello! I am Dexter. I am a kind of computer called a Pokédex. I know facts about all kinds of Pokémon. Pokémon are like animals with special powers.

In this book you will meet some brand-new Pokémon:

Ledyba: These cute Pokémon look like ladybugs! They can fly and have bright red wings with black spots.

Elekid: This Electric Pokémon may look scary, but it's very friendly! Elekid evolves into Electabuzz. It can use Thundershock Attacks just like Pikachu.

Hoothoot: These Flying Pokémon look like owls. They live in trees and only come out at night.

Bellossom: These pretty Grass Pokémon have flowers on top of their heads. They like to sing and dance.

You will also read about many exciting new things about Pokemon you may already know.

Exeggcute: The Egg Pokémon. Exeggcute may look like a bunch of eggs, but it acts more like a group of plant seeds. Exeggcute will attack if it is bothered.

Clefairy: Are friendly and peaceful. They are famous for their magical powers. But they are not easy to find.

Snorlax: It is one of the laziest and biggest Pokémon around. It loves to eat and sleep.

Chansey: These Pokémon bring happiness to their trainers. They carry an egg in a pouch in their bellies.

Chapter One
A GOOD IDEA

"I am bored," Ash Ketchum said. Ash and his friends Misty and Tracey were on a peaceful island. They were resting with their Pokémon. Ash, Misty, and Tracey were all Pokémon trainers. They took care of their Pokémon and taught them new skills.

Usually, there was something exciting happening. But today was quiet. Too quiet for Ash.

"I have an idea," Ash said. "Let's make up a story about our Pokémon."

Tracey took out his sketchpad and a pencil. "That sounds like fun," he said. "I'll draw pictures to go with it."

"How does the story start, Ash?" Misty asked.

Ash thought.

"The story starts on an island just like this one . . ." Ash began.

Chapter Two
TOGEPI TROUBLE

One sunny afternoon, three Pokémon trainers were resting on an island. Their names were Ash, Tracey, and Misty.

The trainers were tired from their long journey.

"Let's take a nap," Ash said.

Ash, Tracey, and Misty stretched out on the grass.

Pikachu and the other Pokémon curled up under a shady tree.

Pikachu closed its eyes. Bulbasaur and Squirtle slept next to Pikachu. Bulbasaur looked like a small dinosaur with a plant bulb on its back. Squirtle looked like a cute turtle.

Tracey's Pokémon napped next to them. Venonat, a purple Bug Pokémon, closed its round, red eyes. Marill, a blue, Water Pokémon, twitched its big, round ears as it slept.

Misty's Psyduck snored through its duck bill. It covered its eyes with its wings.

Only Togepi could not sleep. Togepi was a baby Pokémon. It still wore an eggshell on the bottom of its body. Its tiny arms and legs stuck out of the shell.

Togepi stared up at the bright blue sky.

Suddenly, Togepi got very excited. A swarm of Bug Pokémon was flying across the sky!

Togepi had never seen these Pokémon before. They were red, black, and shiny.

"Togi, togi!" Togepi cried. It hopped away from the other Pokémon. It wanted to play with the new Pokémon.

Togepi hopped across the grass. It hopped to the edge of a hill.

Togepi took one step too many. The little Pokémon tumbled over the hill!

"Togi!" cried Togepi.

Pikachu quickly woke up. Togepi was in trouble!

"Pikachu!" Pikachu woke up the other Pokémon. It ran down the hill.

Togepi rolled into the woods.

Meowth was lost in the same woods. Meowth looked like a cat and was part of Team Rocket. Team Rocket liked to steal Pokémon from other trainers.

Meowth carried a heavy pack on its back.

"I will never find that campground," Meowth grumbled. "Why did Jessie and James want to go camping, anyway? We should be trying to steal Pokémon."

Meowth wanted to stop and rest. But it didn't have a chance.

Togepi rolled right into Meowth! The two Pokémon rolled through the woods together.

They rolled and rolled. Then they fell into a dark hole in the ground!

Pikachu and the others followed Togepi's path. They ran through the woods. They ran up to the hole in the ground.

Pikachu stopped at the hole and

looked down. It looked dark. And deep.

"*Pika?*" Pikachu asked its friends. What should they do?

"*Psy! Psy! Psy!*"

They did not have to decide. Psyduck ran up behind them. It waddled fast so it could catch up.

Psyduck could not stop waddling. It crashed into Pikachu, Bulbasaur, Squirtle, Marill, and Venonat.

All of the Pokémon fell into the hole!

Chapter Three
FLIGHT OF THE LEDYBA

Down, down, down they fell. Pikachu could not see a thing in the dark tunnel.

Then a bright light shone in their eyes. The tunnel opened up. Pikachu and the others tumbled out.

"*Pika!*" Pikachu screamed. They were falling through the sky, next to a big mountain.

Pikachu closed its eyes. It waited to crash into the ground.

Then Pikachu felt something underneath it. Pikachu looked. A swarm of Bug Pokémon was flying beneath them! They looked like ladybugs. They were Ledyba.

One Ledyba caught Pikachu on its back. Other Ledyba caught Bulbasaur, Squirtle, Marill, Venonat, and Psyduck.

The Ledyba soared through the

air. Pikachu looked down at the land below.

Big mountains surrounded them. A waterfall flowed into a crystal blue lake. There was a giant tree next to the lake.

The Ledyba flew down to the giant tree. They rested on some large, green leaves.

Pikachu jumped down from the Ledyba's back. Its friends jumped down, too.

Then the Ledyba flew away.

"Pika!" Pikachu and the other

Pokémon waved good-bye to the helpful Pokémon.

Suddenly, the green leaves began to shake. The leaves were not strong enough to hold the Pokémon.

Crash! Pikachu and the others fell through the leaves. They landed on the soft forest floor.

Dark green plants grew all around them. The brown roots of the giant tree covered the ground.

Pikachu and its friends huddled

together. This place was a little
scary.

"Elekid!"

Pikachu jumped at the sound.

"Elekid!"

A strange Pokémon leaped out
from behind a plant!

Chapter Four

WILL ELEKID HELP?

The strange Pokémon was a little taller than Pikachu. It was orange, with a black lightning bolt on its belly. The top of its head looked like two prongs of a plug.

"Squirtle!" Squirtle put on its

Squirtle Squad sunglasses. When Squirtle was a member of the Squirtle Squad, it used to help other Pokémon whenever there was trouble. Now Squirtle was trying to protect its friends from the new Pokémon.

"Pikachu!" Pikachu told Squirtle. Pikachu was an Electric Pokémon, too, just like Elekid. Maybe they could be friends.

Pikachu ran up to Elekid.

"Pikachu," said Pikachu in a friendly way.

"Elekid," replied the other Pokémon.

Pikachu and Elekid touched hands. An electric spark crackled in the air.

Both Pokémon smiled. The Electric Pokémon had made friends with each other!

Elekid called out to the forest. *"Elekid! Elekid!"*

Slowly, wild Pokémon came out of the shadows. Pikachu had never seen so many wild Pokémon in one place.

Arbok, a purple snake Pokémon, slithered on the ground.

Mankey swung from a tree branch.

Weedle, a hairy Bug Pokémon, crawled out from under a plant.

Magnemite hovered in the air.

A few yellow Weepinbell and Victreebel hung from vines in the tree.

Dugtrio popped out of the dirt.

More Pokémon came out. A pretty Vulpix with soft fur. An Eevee with long, pointy ears. A smiling Clefairy. A Machop with strong muscles. A Lickitung with a long, sticky tongue.

Rattata and Raticate scampered among the tree roots. A chubby, pink Wigglytuff slid down a branch. A smaller Jigglypuff followed right behind it.

"Pika, pika, chu?" Pikachu asked Elekid. Pikachu wanted to know why there were so many wild Pokémon here. Why weren't they afraid of getting captured?

"Ele, ele, elekid," said their new friend. Elekid explained that

no humans lived in this land. Pokémon could live here in peace.

Pikachu smiled. This seemed like a nice place.

Then it remembered why they were here. They needed to find Togepi!

"Pikachu! Pika, pika, pi!" Pikachu told Elekid what Togepi looked like.

Elekid thought. Then tiny sparks glittered on the plug on its head.

"Elekid!" said the Pokémon. Elekid thought it knew where to find Togepi!

Chapter Five
A LONG CLIMB

Elekid led Pikachu and its friends up the giant tree. They walked up sturdy tree branches. They climbed up thick green vines.

The Pokémon did not like climbing up so high. Bulbasaur could not look down. Squirtle tried to keep its balance. It was not easy.

But they had to find Togepi!

As they climbed, more wild Pokémon came out to see them. A big, round Voltorb rolled along the branches. Chansey, a pink Pokémon that carried an egg in a pouch, peeked out to see them. A Parasect with a red mushroom on its back skittled across the leaves.

The Pokémon walked past a hole in the tree trunk.

"Hoothoot!"

A brown, feathered Pokémon

Venonat, Pikachu, Squirtle, Bulbasaur, and Marill are looking for Togepi. Did the baby Pokémon wander into this creepy tunnel?

Whoa! Psyduck is clumsy. It accidentally pushed Pikachu and friends.

Now they're falling into the tunnel, too!

Whew! A group of Ledyba catch Pikachu and friends.
Now they are safe.

But what is this strange place?

Pikachu and the others meet Pokémon they have never seen before. They make a lot of new friends—like Elekid and Bellossom.

A group of Bellossom sings and dances.

Pikachu and friends have to find a missing Exeggcute egg. Maybe it is in this cave, filled with Clefairy.

Or . . . maybe not!

Uh-oh! A storm is coming! Elekid saves a nest of Exeggcute.

The wind is blowing away Togepi's nest. Here comes Pikachu to the rescue!

Togepi is scared.

Time for teamwork. All the Pokémon lend a hand.

Pikachu and Elekid stop the storm with their Thundershock Attacks!

Pikachu, Togepi, Squirtle, Psyduck, Bulbasaur, Marill,
and Venonat say good-bye to their new friends.
They will never forget their rescue adventure.

popped its head out of the hole. It looked like an owl. Pikachu stopped and stared. It had never seen this Pokémon before.

"Hoothoot!" said the Pokémon as Pikachu walked by.

Elekid led Pikachu and the others higher and higher.

Pikachu saw that many large nests rested on the tree branches. Each nest had six eggs in it.

Pikachu looked closer. Each egg had a face! These Pokémon must be Exeggcute.

"Elekid, kid, kid." Elekid ex-

plained that the tree was a safe place for these Pokémon. That's why there were so many Exeggcute nests in the tree.

Elekid pointed to a branch above them.

"Togi, togi!"

Pikachu could not believe it. Togepi was up there!

Pikachu did not wait for the others. It scrambled up the branch.

An Exeggcute nest sat on the end of the branch. And there in the nest was Togepi!

Chapter Six
TOGEPI AND THE EXEGGCUTE

"Pika, pika!" cried Pikachu happily.

"Togi, togi!" replied Togepi. The baby Pokémon sat in the nest with five Exeggcute.

Bulbasaur, Squirtle, Marill, Venonat, and Psyduck caught up to Pikachu. They were all happy to see Togepi.

Bulbasaur opened the plant bulb on its back. Two vines came out. Bulbasaur reached across the nest with the vines. It wanted to get Togepi.

Chomp! One of the Exeggcute bit down on the vine.

"Bulba!" Bulbasaur cried.

Squirtle did not like to see the Exeggcute hurt its friend.

"*Squirtle, squirtle, squirt!*" scolded Squirtle.

But the Exeggcute did not look sorry. They looked angry.

Togepi hopped out of the nest. It wanted to get to Pikachu.

The five Exeggcute hopped after Togepi. They surrounded the baby Pokémon.

The Exeggcute did not want Togepi to leave!

"*Pika, pika?*" Pikachu did not understand why the Exeggcute were so attached to Togepi.

"Elekid, kid," said Elekid.

Elekid reminded Pikachu that Exeggcute are found in groups of six, not five.

One Exeggcute was missing!

Now Pikachu understood. The Exeggcute needed Togepi to make six.

"Pika, pika, pikachu!" Pikachu told its friends.

To get Togepi back, they had to find the missing Exeggcute!

Chapter Seven
DANCE OF THE WILD POKéMON

Elekid led the Pokémon back down the tree.

They were not very happy. It was a long, long way down. And they did not even know where to look!

"Hoothoot!" Hoothoot waved to them as they passed by.

Finally, they reached the forest floor. Elekid led them through a dark passage inside the tree. Many Parasect skittled around.

"Para, para, sect!" they whispered in the dark.

The Pokémon stuck close together. They did not want to get lost.

Elekid kept going. Soon they reached the other end of the tree.

Bright sunlight hit their eyes. They walked into a clearing.

A blue lake sparkled in front of

them. A bubbly waterfall fell into the lake. Tall, grassy ledges circled the clearing.

"Pika!" Pikachu had never seen such a beautiful place.

Then three musical voices filled the air.

"Bela bela bela!"

Three little Pokémon popped out of the grass. They had red flowers on top of their heads. They wore green skirts made of leaves.

Pikachu thought they were so pretty!

The Bellossom began to dance.

More Pokémon popped up on the ledge next to them.

Gloom kicked their tiny legs. Vileplume rose up and down, trying to balance the heavy flowers on their heads.

Then Pikachu saw a splash in the lake. Water Pokémon were joining the dance!

Goldeen and Seaking splashed out of the water. They looked like two goldfish. Then an orange Magikarp flopped up and flipped in the air.

Poliwag and Poliwhirl, the purple Tadpole Pokémon, jumped out of the water. A Tentacool leaped up and waved its tentacles.

On the shore, a Krabby and a Kingler clicked their claws.

Pikachu and its friends hummed along as the Pokémon danced. When the dance was finished, they clapped and clapped.

Then Pikachu remembered. They had to find the missing Exeggcute!

They waved good-bye to the wild Pokémon. Then they went back inside the hollow tree.

Elekid led them to a cave. Soft blue light lit up the rocky walls. Eight pink Clefairy danced on the rocks.

The Clefairy had thick, curly tails and pointy ears.

"Clefairy, clefairy!" they sang as they danced.

Pikachu and the others watched the amazing sight.

Suddenly, the Clefairy began to glow.

Pikachu got nervous. It looked like the Clefairy were building up energy.

Boom! The light from the Clefairy exploded.

The blast sent Pikachu, Elekid, and the other Pokémon flying through the roof of the cave!

Chapter Eight
BOUNCING AROUND

Pikachu and the others rocketed up, up into the sky.

Then they fell back down just as quickly.

Bounce! They each landed on a springy green leaf.

Bulbasaur, Squirtle, Marill,

Venonat, and Psyduck were happy to be safe on the ground.

But Pikachu and Elekid liked the bouncy leaves.

Boing! Pikachu bounced up to a higher leaf. Elekid did the same.

Boing! They bounced again and landed on leaves even higher.

"Pi. Ka. Chu!" Pikachu was having a great time.

"E. Le. Kid!" Elekid was having fun, too.

Boing! They bounced a third time.

But they bounced too high!

They sailed across the sky.

Pikachu saw that they were fly-ing toward a waterfall.

But something was in their way. Meowth! The furry Pokémon was stuck on a tall tree branch. It had landed in the tree when it fell through the hole with Togepi.

"Watch where you're going!" snapped Meowth.

But Pikachu and Elekid were out of control. They banged into Meowth.

Meowth fell from the tree branch. Now all three Pokémon started to fall to the ground below.

"Pikaaaa!" yelled Pikachu. It looked like they were going to crash.

Then *boing*! They bounced again.

This time they did not bounce on a leaf. They bounced on the belly of a wild Snorlax!

The sleeping Snorlax did not even wake up. Pikachu, Elekid, and Meowth bounced on its big belly. Then they went flying up into the waterfall!

This time, they did not bounce. They landed on the hard back of Gyarados. This blue Pokémon looked like a large, scary sea monster.

Gyarados did not like having the Pokémon on its back. It roared. Then it swam up the waterfall.

Pikachu, Elekid, and Meowth tried to hang on.

Meowth was angry. "Look what you did, you little yellow rat!" Meowth told Pikachu.

That made Pikachu angry. Without thinking, Pikachu shocked Meowth with an electric blast.

The shock made Meowth's fur stand on end. The shock also hit Gyarados. The big Pokémon lost its balance. It tumbled down the waterfall.

Pikachu, Elekid, and Meowth could not hold on any longer!

Chapter Nine
SAVE THE NESTS!

Meowth flew high into the sky.

"It looks like I am blasting off again!" said Meowth.

Pikachu and Elekid flew in another direction. They landed safely on the soft forest floor.

Pikachu's friends ran toward them. Squirtle, Bulbasaur, Marill,

Venonat, and Psyduck were glad that Pikachu was all right.

But they were also worried. Dark clouds were covering the sky. A strong wind was blowing.

"Bulba, bulbasaur," said Bulbasaur. It was worried that the Exeggcute nests would not be safe.

"Pika, pika, pi," answered Pikachu. It thought they should make sure Togepi and all the Exeggcute were all right.

The others agreed. They ran back to the big tree. They climbed up the branches.

Rain poured from the sky. Wind whipped against their faces.

Soon they came to the Exeggcute nests. The strong wind was carrying them away!

"Pikachu!" cried Pikachu. They had to save the nests.

Each Pokémon found a nest and held on tight. Pikachu climbed to the highest branch. It grabbed on to the nest that held Togepi.

"Togi, togi!" Togepi was happy to see its friend.

The wind blew harder and harder. The Pokémon struggled to

keep the nests from blowing away.
But it looked like they might lose
them.

"Pikaaaaa!" cried Pikachu. It
would not give up.

The wild Pokémon heard
Pikachu's cry. They came out of
their safe homes to help.

Slowbro helped Squirtle.

Sandshrew helped Venonat.

Mankey helped Bulbasaur.

Pidgeot and Vulpix helped
Marill.

Machop helped Elekid.

Together, they held on tightly to

the nests. They tried to move them to a safer spot.

A round, pink Wigglytuff hopped up to the top branch to help Pikachu. It grabbed the other side of the nest.

Even Snorlax came to help! It held Wigglytuff so it would not blow away.

Pikachu smiled. With all the Pokémon helping, the nests would be safe!

Then *crack*! Thunder boomed. Lightning lit up the sky.

A lightning bolt struck a nearby

tree branch. The branch crashed to the ground.

Crack! Another lightning bolt struck. Pikachu watched another tree branch fall.

Pikachu had to think fast. The lightning was very powerful. All of the Pokémon were in terrible danger!

Chapter Ten
A CHAIN OF POKÉMON

Pikachu knew what to do. It had to get to the highest part of the tree.

Elekid and Machop made sure their nest was safe. They joined Wigglytuff and Snorlax. They grabbed Togepi's nest.

Psyduck held on to the nest, too.

Pikachu ran up to the very top of the tree.

Thunder boomed. Another lightning bolt flashed in the sky.

"Pikachuuuuu!" Pikachu aimed a Thundershock Attack at the lightning. Pikachu's electric charge hit the lightning bolt. It stopped the lightning bolt from hitting the tree.

Boom! Another lightning bolt flashed.

Pikachu sent up another Thundershock.

Elekid ran up the tree to help Pikachu. The two Electric Pokémon aimed blast after blast of electricity at the lightning.

Bam! Pikachu and Elekid aimed one big blast at the storm clouds.

The powerful blast sent sparks flying onto the tree leaves. A fire broke out!

Squirtle and Marill squirted water from their mouths. They put out the flames.

Pikachu and Elekid had stopped the lightning. But a strong wind still rocked the tree branches.

"Togi, togi!" Togepi called up to Pikachu.

Suddenly, a strong gust of wind swept up from below.

Togepi's nest flew off the tree branch.

"Bulba!" Bulbasaur acted fast. It reached out and grabbed the nest with its vines.

The strong wind tugged at the nest. Bulbasaur needed help.

Machop grabbed on to Bul-basaur.

Venonat grabbed on to Machop.

Squirtle grabbed on to Venonat.

The others joined in, making a chain of Pokémon. Pidgeot, Marill, Wigglytuff, Vulpix, Sandshrew, and Slowbro all grabbed on.

Pikachu and Elekid ran down from the top of the tree. Elekid grabbed on to Slowbro. Pikachu grabbed on to Elekid.

Psyduck tried to grab on to Pikachu. But it fell flat on its face!

Snorlax reached out with its big paw and held Pikachu.

The Pokémon pulled with all their might. They tried to pull the nest back onto the ground.

The wind blew harder and faster. Leaves whipped by. Apples blew off the trees.

Snorlax watched the apples fly by. Snorlax was always hungry. And the apples looked yummy.

Snorlax let go of Pikachu. It tried to catch an apple.

"Pikaaaaaaa!" yelled Pikachu.

The chain of Pokémon was blowing away!

Chapter Eleven
PIKACHU SAVES THE DAY

Pikachu chomped down on a scraggly tree stump. It held the stump tightly between its teeth. The chain of Pokémon waved in the air like a flag.

"Bulbasaur!" The Grass Poké-

mon tried hard to hold the nest
with its vines.

Pikachu could not hold on much
longer, either. The wind was blowing hard.

"Pikaaa!" The wind pulled
Pikachu off the tree stump.

Just in time, Snorlax remembered that its friends needed help.
It grabbed Pikachu.

One by one, Snorlax pulled the
Pokémon back down.

Finally, Snorlax grabbed
Bulbasaur.

But it was too late. Bulbasaur lost its grip. The wind tossed the nest in the air!

In a flash, Pikachu ran up Bulbasaur's vines. It held the end of a vine in one hand. It grabbed the nest in the other.

Snorlax pulled down Bulbasaur and then Pikachu. Snorlax set the nest down gently in the cradle of the tree branch.

The Pokémon cheered. The nests were all right! They saved Togepi and all the Exeggcute.

At that moment, the wind and

rain stopped. The dark clouds blew away.

A colorful rainbow appeared in the blue sky. Then a beautiful Flying Pokémon flew across the rainbow. The blue Pokémon had a long, flowing tail.

"*Pika.*" Pikachu had never seen anything like it.

"*Togi, togi!*" Togepi hopped out of the nest and hugged Pikachu.

Pikachu was so happy!

"*Exeggcute! Exeggcute!*" The five Exeggcute hopped out of the nest and followed Pikachu. They still did not want Togepi to leave them.

"*Pika,*" groaned Pikachu.

They saved the nests.

But they had not found the missing Exeggcute.

How would they ever get Togepi back home?

Chapter Twelve
EXEGGUTOR!

"Pikachu," Pikachu told the other Pokémon. They had to try to get Togepi home. Ash, Misty, and Tracey would be worried about them.

They followed Elekid back down the tree. Togepi toddled along next to Pikachu. The Exeggcute hopped after them. They grumbled angrily the whole way.

The wild Pokémon watched Pikachu and the others as they walked. Soon they reached the ground.

"Exeggcute! Exeggcute!"

The Exeggcute formed a circle around Togepi. They would not let the baby Pokémon leave them.

Pikachu sighed. It did not know what to do. They might have to stay in this land forever. Pikachu already missed Ash.

Just then, a pink Pokémon

popped out from behind a leaf.
A Chansey.

"Chansey. Chansey," said the
Pokémon in a sweet voice.

Chansey took an egg out of its
pouch. It put the egg on the
ground.

But it wasn't an egg. It was the
missing Exeggcute!

"Exeggcute! Exeggcute!" the
other Exeggcute bounced up and
down happily.

The six Exeggcute jumped and
bounced. Then a bright white light
shone around them.

Pikachu could not believe its eyes. The Exeggcute were evolving!

The light flashed. The Exeggcute disappeared. In their place stood a Pokémon with three yellow heads.

All three Exeggutor faces smiled. The Pokémon danced on its two thick legs.

"Elekid. Ele, ele," said Elekid. It explained that the Exeggcute needed the missing egg so that they could evolve.

"Pikachu!" said Pikachu. It was happy the Exeggutor evolved. And now they could take Togepi home.

Elekid looked a little sad. It did not want its new friends to leave.

"Pika, pika," said Pikachu. It would not forget Elekid. Or any of the wild Pokémon here.

Elekid smiled.

Elekid led Pikachu and the others to a big mountain. Snorlax, Exeggutor, Chansey, and a bunch of Exeggcute came along to say good-bye.

Elekid pointed to a hole in the side of the mountain. Pikachu and the others climbed up a path. They reached the hole.

Pikachu waved to Elekid and its new friends below.

"Elekid!"

"Snorlax!"

"Chansey!"

"Exeggutor!"

"Exeggcute!" called the Pokémon.

"Pikachuuuu!" Pikachu replied. Its voice rang through the mountains.

Pikachu and its friends entered the passage . . .

. . . and came out in the middle of a lake!

Pikachu looked around. They were back where they started. Ash, Tracey, and Misty still napped on the shore.

Nearby, Meowth floated to the top of the water. The scratch cat Pokémon had made it back, too.

"I am never going camping again!" said Meowth.

Pikachu and the others splashed in the cool water. On shore, Ash

yawned and stretched. Misty and
Tracey opened their eyes.

"Look," Ash said. "Our Pokémon
are playing in the water."

Pikachu paddled back to
shore. It was so good to see Ash
again.

"Did you have a nice rest?" Ash
asked Pikachu.

A nice rest! Pikachu was very
tired from the rescue adventure.
So many things had happened.

They saw brand-new Pokémon.

They made new friends.

They rescued Togepi.

They saw Exeggcute evolve into Exeggutor.

They had a great day.

But it was good to be back!

Pikachu hugged Ash.

"Pikachu!"

Chapter Thirteen
YOU NEVER KNOW!

"And Pikachu never forgot its amazing rescue adventure," Ash said. "The end."

"That was a pretty good story, Ash," Misty said.

Tracey held up his sketchpad. He had drawn a great picture of the Exeggcute turning into Exeggutor.

"What do you think?" Tracey asked.

"That's great!" Ash said. "It's so good, I bet somebody will turn our story into a real book some day."

Misty laughed. "In your dreams, Ash," she said. "That'll never happen."

Ash shrugged. "Who knows?" he said. "You never know."